MOLLY O'GRADY'S HOME RUN

The N.Y. Bombers loses the World Series to its arch rival, but Molly hits the home run for retirement in sunny Florida

STEPHEN R. CHAMPI

outskirtspress

DENVER, COLORADO

Molly O'Grady's Home Run
The N.Y. Bombers loses the World Series to its arch rival,
but Molly hits the home run for retirement in sunny Florida

Outskirts Press, Inc.
http://www.outskirtspress.com

ISBN: 978-1-4787-2074-4

PRINTED IN THE UNITED STATES OF AMERICA

MOLLY O'GRADY'S HOME RUN

The seventh and last game of the NY Subway World Series ended with the NY Stars beating its cross-town rival, the NY Bombers, for the World Baseball Championship. It was the first time in Major League history that an expansion team of the National League had defeated the Bombers in a World Series competition.

The baseball stadium rocked with thunderous cheering as thousands of Stars fans ran onto the playing field, wildly celebrating their team's victory. A celebration was also beginning in the Stars' locker room as jubilant players were squirting and dousing each other with champagne.

However, a different scene prevailed in the Bombers' locker room. Players quietly showered and dressed while their manager, John T. O'Grady, sat morose and dejected in his office, unavailable to the media for post-game comments.

For Bombers fans, the stunning loss to the Stars was due to the tragic beaning of Jackie LaMar, the Bombers' team captain, star shortstop, and its most valuable player, by a 100 MPH fastball in the All-Star Game that ended LaMar's career.

On the morning of the crucial seventh game of the series, millions of baseball fans throughout the nation anxiously awaited the start of the game. Bombers fans were hoping for a record-setting sixth consecutive World Series victory, while Stars fans were rooting for bragging rights in upsetting the mighty Bombers. However, one loyal Bombers fan was silently wishing that the Stars would win. Molly O'Grady, for the first time in forty-two years of marriage to her husband, wanted the Bombers to lose. Her guilty feelings were overcome by a desire for life retirement in sunny Florida.

Molly knew John would never voluntarily retire from the game of baseball, unless he were incapacitated, or party to an event that tarnished his baseball image, reputation, and legacy.

Shortly after John left for the stadium for the deciding game of the series, Molly lifted her head skyward, closed her eyes, and asked for a Stars victory in winning the world championship, along with asking for forgiveness for being so disloyal to her husband.

Hours after the game ended and everyone had left the stadium, John O'Grady, discouraged and fatigued, fell asleep in a deep dream. Suddenly, out of the darkness of the dream appeared Ted Daniels, O'Grady's best friend, his boss, the general manager of the NY Bombers. O'Grady rubbed his eyes in disbelief and said, "Ted, is it really you?"

"Yes, John. I come with great news. I found the baseball player to replace LaMar next season and help the Bombers win its record-setting twenty-eighth league championship, the World Series, and your election to the Baseball Hall of Fame."

Stunned by the news, O'Grady responded, "Really, Ted?"

"Yes, John. The player is waiting outside your office to meet with you."

O'Grady rose half out of his desk chair in excitement. "For heaven's sake, show him in."

Daniels returned, accompanied by a tall, athletic blonde female. O'Grady gasped in bewilderment. Catching his breath, he uttered in a critical tone, "Ted, is this some sort of a joke?"

"No, John, I have never been more serious. This girl is a natural. She is the ideal person to replace LaMar. She can hit for power, run with speed, throw with distance and accuracy, field with range, and bunt with consistency."

"Ted, be reasonable. Baseball will never permit women to play in the major leagues with men."

"Why? Because of their biological, physical, and characteristic differences? John, women are no longer the typical small, fragile, and delicate females of past generations. Today female players have proven their superior athleticism in both amateur and professional sports."

"Ted, but this doesn't prove that women are ready and capable of playing major league baseball alongside men."

"Yes, it does. Provided deserving female athletes are given a fair opportunity to compete, and receive the same training and development that men do."

"But why the major leagues, instead of some less-demanding professional sport?"

"For several reasons. From the women's perspective, major league baseball represents the logical

venue for the next giant step in furthering their his-
torical movement for attaining incredible changes
in gender parity, social freedoms, working rights,
and a better quality of life. Major league baseball
will offer female athletes a showcase for their abil-
ity and right to achieve stardom, fame, glory, and
wealth."

"Ted, do you really believe that the timing is right
for millions of baseball fans to accept the entry of
women into the major leagues?"

"Yes, but it won't be easy. To a large extent success
will depend upon public opinion, the extent of social backlash, and how fairly the media reports the
event."

"How will the Baseball Commissioner, team owners, and men players react?"

"The commissioner and team owners will unite in
solid protest and opposition. Players will engage
in ridicule and sexist jokes. However, momentum
of a national female movement in favor of women
players, coupled with the influence and power of
public opinion, along with substantial increases in
baseball revenue and profits, will carry the day."

"And you want me and the Bombers to initiate the
transition of female players into the major leagues

by beginning with the replacement of Jackie LaMar with your female phenomenon?"

"Yes. And in doing so, John, you will become more famous in baseball history than Branch Rickey for Jackie Robinson's entry into the major leagues that struck down racial discrimination in professional baseball."

"Fancy words, Ted, but I'm interested only in winning next year's World Series -- not in becoming a scapegoat and traitor in baseball history."

"John, if the transition is a failure, as general manager, I'll take the blame, and if it is a success, then you can take the credit."

"Fair enough. All right, Ted. Bring your prospect to the stadium tomorrow morning at 7:00 for a tryout, on one strict condition. No one is to be told of this event -- especially not the media."

At 7:00 the following morning, the only persons in the stadium were O'Grady, Daniels, the young prospect, and three Bomber coaches to assist in the tryout session.

After a warmup period, O'Grady was anxious to begin. He took command. In a rasping voice he barked, "Jim, you take first base. Clyde, you hit.

Mike, you catch for Clyde. Ted, you and I will station ourselves in the third base coaching box." Then he looked straight at the young woman. It was the first time in his long baseball career that he had to summon courage to address a ballplayer. Softly and slowly he said, "All right, Miss, go out to short and show us what you can do." She nodded and dashed to the shortstop position, stationing herself deep in the infield with her spikes caressing the outfield grass. She then moved a shade to her left, crouched, glued her eyes on home plate, and waited.

Crack! Fungo and horsehide met! The ball, a grass cutter, sharply hit, traveled at a crazy rate of speed. It was scooped up cleanly, thrown to first in a deft, effortless style. From beginning to completion, the play had been executed in a minimum of time and motion. It had been perfection, sheer perfection!

In the next hour, the young woman was tested in all phases of the game. They made her go deep to her right, then to her left. She handled pop-ups, line-drives and high, lazy, twisting foul flies.

Batting came in the second hour. She was made to bunt, hit away. Then hit to right, then to left. She was thrown fastballs, curves, knucklers, screwballs, sliders, and change-ups. They threw her high, then low; inside and outside.

Finally, O'Grady had had enough. Beyond gender problems, she possessed grace, speed, skill and coordination, and was ready to play major league baseball.

The girl was batting when O'Grady turned his back to the plate and whispered, "Okay, Ted -- you win."

O'Grady never heard the warning yell. The ball struck him just below the base of the skull. He immediately fell unconscious.

In his dream, O'Grady felt no pain, only a sharp ringing in his ears. Suddenly, his eyes opened and he slowly became aware that the phone had been ringing. He lifted the receiver. Too late. The party had hung up!

O'Grady slumped in his office chair, disoriented, shaking his head, cleaning his head, and thankful that he experienced only a bad dream.

Slowly, he began digesting the enormity of the dream and what the consequences would be on the American public, society in general, the national past time, the male-female relationship, his beloved Bombers team, the team's ownership and organization, not to mention his personal baseball status, reputation, and legacy.

"My god... Women playing in the major leagues," he whispered out loud to himself. The disruption in the game would be immense and incalculable. Impacting all important segments of the nation. The media would have a field day. The women's TV program called "the View" alone would be responsible in stirring up all type of controversy. Late night TV shows like David Letterman and Jay Leno would make countless bad jokes about women and their femininity. Major newspapers throughout the country would run pro and con editorials and publish untold of pieces from women groups, gays, sociologists, psychologists, sport commentators and agents, The Baseball Commissioner, club owners, and loyal baseball fans.

O'Grady had enough. "This is crazy. After all, it was only a horrible dream. It couldn't be true in a million years. Why am I letting it get to me? I wonder what Molly's reaction would be? Perhaps it would be best if I made believe that the dream never took place." He then showered, dressed, and started for home.

O'Grady encountered heavy traffic in driving home, and all during the way he had this nagging feeling that he should tell Molly about his dream.

When O'Grady arrived home, Molly had kept supper warm as she had done on hundreds of other occasions. She never questioned his tardiness or details of the lost game. She knew from experience that in his own good time John would eventually tell her about the game. He always did.

Molly at dinner became keenly aware that John was troubled. She thought that it was due to losing today's game, and what the loss meant to his not becoming the first manager in major league history to win six consecutive world series championships. However, she knew from the past that John would bide his time and eventually tell her what was troubling him.

"John, you're not eating." Are you that disappointed in losing today's game?"

"No, Molly, its not in losing today's game but some weird event that happened to me after the game when I was all alone in my office after everyone had gone home."

"Want to talk about it?"

"Not now. Maybe later."

Later in the evening after John had settled down having his coffee in his favorite lounge chair in the den he summoned the courage to tell Molly the event of his dream and anxiously awaited her reaction.

"John, you shouldn't allow yourself to become so unnerved over a silly dream that will never effect your baseball career even if it becomes a reality."

"Why not, Molly?"

"Because of the timing factor. Women will never become major league baseball players at any time during your active baseball career. Although American women have made great progress in achieving gender equality in common and in parallel with men in today's technological society it is not a top priority for women to play major league baseball players instead of becoming President of the United States."

"Rest assured, John, you will long be an honored member of the baseball Hall of Fame before any woman is playing major league baseball. However, you can protect now you baseball career and eventual election to the Hall of Fame very simply."

"How, Molly?"

"Doesn't a rule of the Hall of Fame require that a player or manager must be out of baseball for a minimum of five years before becoming eligible for election to and admission into the Hall?"

"True, Molly."

"Then you should retire from baseball very soon. It will be more than five years before a woman plays major league baseball if your dream comes true."

At bedtime, John thanked Molly for being so helpful and understanding, Molly sympathetically and with a compassionate smile kissed her husband good night. John fell asleep dreaming of his cherished nomination to the Baseball Hall of Fame. Meanwhile, Molly once again looked skyward and silently thanked Providence, because tomorrow she knew that John would hold a press conference notifying the sporting world of his retirement from baseball.

The End